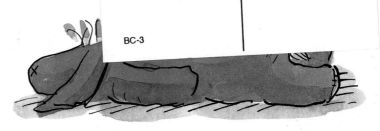

For Sue and Rosemary
for all their help

Published 1993 by Thomasson-Grant, Inc.
First published 1993 by ABC (All Books for Children),
a division of The All Children's Company Ltd., London.
Text and illustrations © 1993 Selina Young

00 99 98 97 96 95 94 93   5 4 3 2 1

Library of Congress Cataloging-in-Publication Data
Young, Selina.
Ned / Selina Young.
p. cm.
Summary: Emily and her constant companion, a green donkey named Ned, head off
to real school for the first time and make an interesting discovery.
ISBN 1-56566-033-1
[1. Toys—Fiction. 2. Schools—Fiction.] I. Title
PZ7.Y8792Ne 1993
[E]—dc20   92-33518
CIP
AC

Thomasson-Grant, Inc.
One Morton Drive
Charlottesville, VA 22903-6806
(804) 977-1780

NED

Selina Young

Thomasson-Grant
Charlottesville, Virginia

Ned was a lumpy green
donkey who walked
with a wobble.

He was Emily's donkey, and
they went everywhere together.

When it was time to eat,
Ned sat next to Emily on top of lots
of cushions. "It's Ned's
idea," Emily told
her parents,
"but I agree."

Every morning when Emily and Ned
woke up, they gave a big yawn. Then
Emily got dressed while Ned waited.

Sometimes they went straight
downstairs for breakfast.

But other days there were dragons waiting
in the hall, so Emily and Ned stopped to
fight them. "It's Ned's idea," Emily
told her parents, "but I agree."
Emily and Ned always
won, although Mom
usually had to call
them a few times.

fearsome dragon.

But today was special. Today Emily was going to school. So when Mom shouted, "Breakfast, Emily!" they went straight downstairs. "It's a good thing there aren't any dragons today," Emily told Ned. Ned thought the dragons might just be hiding especially well, but there wasn't time to look.

Emily and Ned usually had juice, cornflakes, and milk, but they weren't hungry this morning. "It's Ned's idea, but I agree. Maybe he's a little scared to start school," Emily explained to Mom and Dad. "I won't make him eat today."

But Mom said Emily had to
eat something, so she had milk
and toast.

Then Dad said, "School time!"
Emily wasn't absolutely sure she
wanted to go, but Mom had all her new
things ready. "You'll have fun, Emily."

So Emily put on her hat
and coat, stuffed Ned into
her bag, and off they
went with Dad.

The classroom was full. "This will be your coat hook, Emily," said Mrs. Zipper.

Emily's Dad said good-bye. "Mom will pick you up when school is over," he said, and he gave her a quick kiss.

The first day of school can be scary for a little lumpy donkey. "Don't be afraid," Emily whispered to Ned. "I'm right here." And she gave him a quick kiss.

Mrs. Zipper was very good at helping with painting, buttons, reading, paper cut-outs, making things from cardboard, rolling up sleeves, giving little hugs if you were sad (Emily was sure to give Ned a little hug, too), or cleaning up a mess.

Emily and Ned joined in everything.

When Mrs. Zipper rang a bell, Emily thought it was time to go home. "No," explained Mrs. Zipper. "This isn't the going-home bell. This is the lunch bell. Everyone take your lunch box, line up, and follow me."

Emily didn't see Ned slip off
his chair onto the floor.

After lunch, everyone went to the playground.
Emily felt that something was wrong, but when
she checked, she had her hat, and her mittens,
her ladybug purse and . . .

where was Ned?

"Mrs. Zipper, I've lost Ned! Have you seen him?"
Mrs. Zipper hadn't, but she called out, "Emily can't find her little green donkey.
Everyone look!"

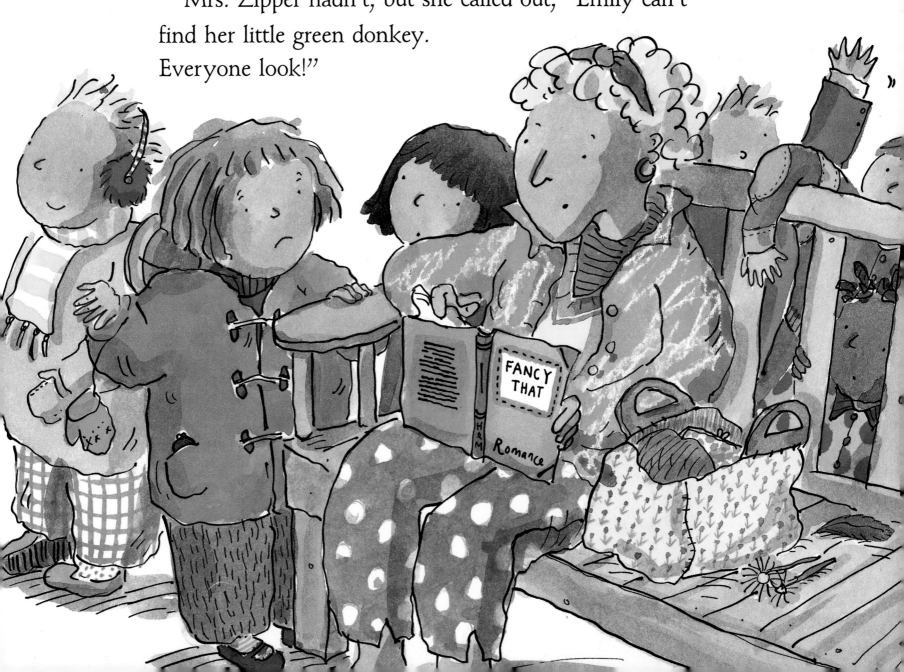

And they did.

Under the swings, by the merry-go-round, and in the cafeteria (they even asked the serving ladies).

They looked in the classroom, inside the dressing-up box, in the book rack, by the goldfish bowl, in the toybox, in the corner house—even in Mrs. Zipper's pencil drawer, where no one except Mrs. Zipper was supposed to look. Emily felt a big lump in her throat getting bigger. Just then someone shouted, "Here! He's here!"

And there he was.
A little dusty and a little
cold, but still a little
green donkey.

Emily hugged him
tightly. "Oh, Ned."

Emily held Ned for the rest of the day.
And when Mom came to get her, Emily
made sure he was safely in her bag as she told
Mom all about Ned's adventure.

"It sounds as though you and Ned might each have had a better day if he'd been home," said Mom.

Emily looked at Ned, but she didn't say anything.

That night, Emily and Ned went to bed right after dinner.

"Ned is tired, and so am I," Emily told her parents.

Mom and Dad tucked them in.

Ned made Emily look under the covers to be sure the dragons hadn't gotten in while they'd been at school. "Ned says he feels safest here," said Emily. "Look! He's asleep already."

The next day when Emily's Mom called her for breakfast, Emily came downstairs alone. "Ned is staying home today," she told her parents. "I'll miss him, but he's going to keep the dragons out of my bedroom."

"Whose idea was that?" asked Dad.

"Mine," answered Emily.

"But Ned agrees."